FERGUS AND ZEKE

AND THE 100TH DAY OF SCHOOL

KATE MESSNER

ILLUSTRATED BY HEATHER ROSS

CANDLEWICK PRESS

FOR ADRIANNA
KM

FOR TC, WHO DOES THE COUNTING
HR

Text copyright © 2021 by Kate Messner
Illustrations copyright © 2021 by Heather Ross

First edition 2021

Library of Congress Catalog Card Number pending
ISBN 978-1-5362-1300-3

21 22 23 24 25 26 CCP 10 9 8 7 6 5 4 3 2 1

Printed in Shenzhen, Guangdong, China

This book was typeset in Minion.
The illustrations were created digitally.

Candlewick Press
99 Dover Street
Somerville, Massachusetts 02144

www.candlewick.com

A JUNIOR LIBRARY GUILD SELECTION

CONTENTS

CHAPTER 1

ONE HUNDRED GREAT IDEAS
• 1 •

CHAPTER 2

ONE HUNDRED IMPOSSIBLE CHALLENGES
• 13 •

CHAPTER 3

A STORY IN ONE HUNDRED WORDS
• 27 •

CHAPTER 4

NINETY-NINE AND A HALF CHEESE PUFFS
• 37 •

ONE HUNDRED GREAT IDEAS

FERGUS AND ZEKE loved being the class pets in Miss Maxwell's room. When Miss Maxwell started the day with music, Fergus and Zeke sang along. When the children wrote stories, Fergus and Zeke wrote stories, too. And when the class studied weather, Fergus and Zeke made up their own forecast.

Miss Maxwell kept a big calendar at the front of the room. Some of the days on the calendar had stars. Those were the special days her class loved best of all. Fergus and Zeke loved them, too.

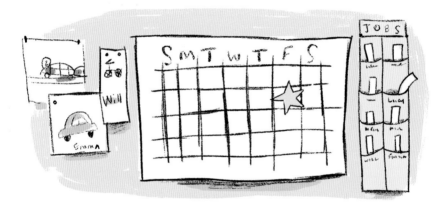

They made fancy fall hats to celebrate the first day of autumn.

They dressed up for the costume parade on Halloween.

And they cut tissue-paper snowflakes on the first day of winter.

One day, Miss Maxwell told her students, "We have been working and playing together as a class for a long time now. Almost one hundred days!" She pointed to a star on her calendar. "On Friday, we will have a party to mark our one hundredth day of school."

"How will we celebrate?" asked Jake.

"By using the number one hundred in as many ways as we can. For example, we might sing a song with one hundred words," said Miss Maxwell. "Or share one hundred pretzels as a snack."

"We should have one hundred cupcakes!" said Neela.

"One hundred pizzas!" said Will.

"I'm afraid that might give you one hundred tummy aches," said Miss Maxwell.

"How about one hundred days without homework?" said Emma.

Miss Maxwell laughed. "By Friday, I'd like each of you to bring in a collection of one hundred items so that we can see what one hundred looks like. We will paint a One Hundredth Day of School banner and make a big display for our celebration." She handed out crayons and paper. "Today, we will make some art to put up on the wall for our party. Please draw a picture of what you think you will look like when you are one hundred years old."

"When I am one hundred years old, I will have a great big family," said Will.

"When I am one hundred years old, I will have white hair and a fancy cane," said Emma.

"When I am one hundred years old, I will do whatever I want," said Neela.

"What do you think we will look like when we are one hundred years old?" Fergus asked.

"We will look fabulous!" said Zeke. "By the time we are one hundred years old, we will be famous."

"And we will still be best friends," said Fergus.

While Miss Maxwell taped the pictures to the wall, the class brainstormed ideas for their hundredth-day collections.

"I have a lot of books at home," said Emma. "Maybe I'll bring one hundred books!"

"I have a rock collection," said Neela. "Maybe I'll bring one hundred rocks!"

"I love books and rocks," Miss Maxwell said. "But don't forget that you will have to carry your one hundred things to school. You will want to choose something smaller."

"This project sounds like fun!" Zeke said.

"It does," said Fergus. "But I do not think we have one hundred of anything."

"Don't worry," said Zeke. "I will have one hundred great ideas by tomorrow."

CHAPTER 2

ONE HUNDRED IMPOSSIBLE CHALLENGES

The next morning, the children lined up for gym class. "Ms. Khan has some fun challenges to get you ready for Friday!" Miss Maxwell said.

Fergus and Zeke loved challenges. So they climbed out of their cage and jumped into Emma's gym bag to tag along.

Ms. Khan had set up special stations in the gym.

Neela and Jake decided they would try to kick one hundred soccer goals.

Emma wanted to shoot one hundred baskets.

Will chose to hula-hoop for one hundred seconds.

And Lucy tried to jump rope one hundred times without stopping.

HULA -HOOP FOR 100 seconds

"That looks like fun!" Zeke said. "Let's go!"

But all of the challenges were BIG.

Fergus and Zeke couldn't lift the basketball.

Or the Hula-Hoop.

When they tried the soccer challenge, they almost got kicked into the goal along with the ball.

"We need a mouse-size challenge."
Fergus looked around until he found a piece
of string in the corner of the gym. "Now we
can jump rope like Lucy!"

"You go first," Zeke said. "I will count."

So Fergus started jumping.

"One . . . two . . . three . . . four . . ." Zeke
counted. He counted all the way to sixty-
five. Then Fergus tripped.

"You have to start all over now," Zeke said.

Fergus tried again. And again. And again. But he never made it to one hundred.

"That was a good try," Zeke said. "One hundred is a very big number when you are jumping rope."

* * *

When they got back to Miss Maxwell's room, Zeke had a new idea. "I'm going to run one hundred miles on our spinny wheel!" He jumped on and started running.

"One hundred is a very big number when you're counting miles," Fergus said. "How will you know when you are finished?"

"I'm not sure," Zeke said. He was already out of breath. "Do you think I'm close?"

"I'm afraid not," Fergus said.

Zeke stepped off the spinny wheel. "We need a new idea."

Fergus agreed. "One that is not so tiring."

"I know!" Zeke said. He set a timer. "We will take a nap for one hundred seconds."

Fergus and Zeke got all cozy in their wood chips. Fergus was just starting to doze when the timer went off.

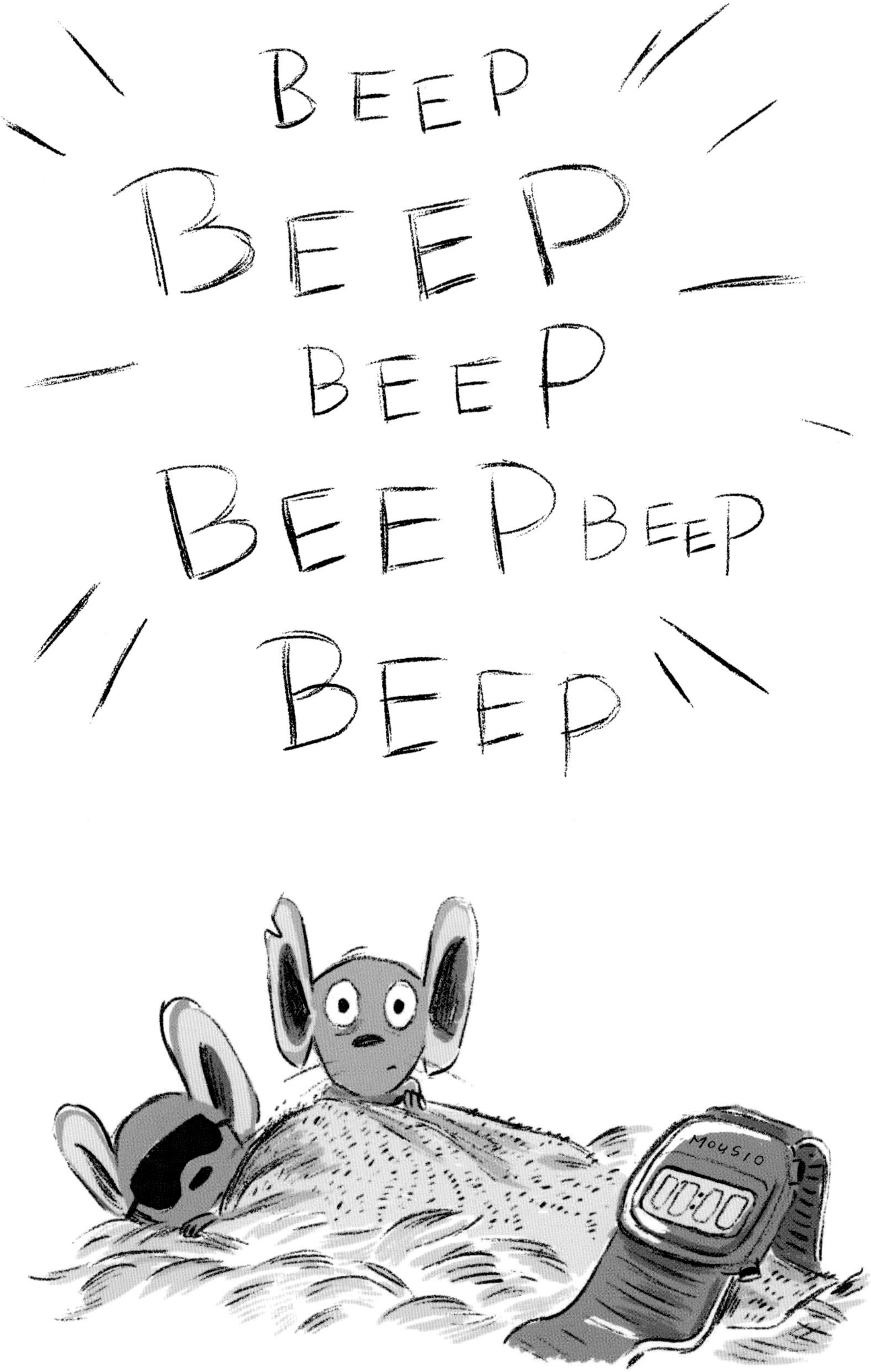
BEEP
BEEP
BEEP
BEEP BEEP
BEEP
MOUSIO
00:00

"That was a mighty quick nap," Fergus said.

Zeke yawned. "One hundred is a very small number when you are trying to snooze."

* * *

After lunch, Miss Maxwell's class had sharing time. Some of the students had already brought in their collections.

Neela had built a tower of one hundred blocks.

Emma had folded sixty of the one hundred paper airplanes she hoped to make.

And Lucy had brought in one hundred cheese puffs.

"Yum!" said Zeke. "This project makes me hungry."

"This project makes me sad," said Fergus. "We still don't have an idea."

"We could make a tower like Neela's!" said Zeke.

"We do not have one hundred blocks," said Fergus.

"No. I guess we don't," Zeke said. He looked around. "But we might have one hundred wood chips!"

Zeke began stacking the wood chips on top of one another. "One . . . two . . . three . . ."

Fergus helped. But when they got to forty-seven, their wood-chip pile started to teeter.

"Watch out!" said Zeke.

CRASH!

"We didn't even get halfway to one hundred," Fergus said sadly.

"One hundred is a very big number when you are stacking wood chips," Zeke said. "We will have to try a new idea tomorrow."

CHAPTER 3
A STORY IN ONE HUNDRED WORDS

The next morning, the class had writing workshop. "Today we will write stories to get ready for the one hundredth day of school," Miss Maxwell said. "Each story should be exactly one hundred words long."

Fergus and Zeke loved stories. They couldn't wait for sharing time to see what the children wrote.

Will's story was about a boy who had a pet dragon. One day, his dragon ran away. The boy had to search all over the kingdom to find him.

Lucy's story was about a funny bear who couldn't find his shoes. He looked for them everywhere. At the end, it turned out he was wearing them the whole time!

Emma stood up and read her story next. "Once upon a time there was an amazing astronaut named Emma . . ."

Fergus and Zeke sat on their wood chips and listened. The story was very exciting.

Emma the astronaut got trapped in outer space! Her rocket was broken, and she was all alone. At the end, she came up with a plan to get home just in time.

"The end," Emma read, and closed her notebook.

"That was exactly one hundred words," Fergus said. He had been keeping count. "Zeke, we should write a one-hundred-word story, too. That could be our special project for the one hundredth day of school."

"Great idea!" Zeke said. "I will write the words, and you can draw the pictures. It will be the best story ever."

Fergus and Zeke gathered their writing and art supplies and set to work.

"Once upon a time there was a mouse named Fergus," Zeke wrote. "Fergus had a big problem. A terrible monster wanted to eat him for lunch!"

"I do not think I like this story," said Fergus.

"Don't worry," said Zeke. "It will all be okay in the end. But first there has to be doom and disaster." He handed Fergus a pencil. "Draw a picture of the terrible monster."

"Should I draw myself, too?" Fergus asked.

"Yes," Zeke said. "Running away and screaming."

Fergus drew while Zeke wrote some more.

"Fergus ran away. He ran into the woods and up a mountain. On top of the mountain was a deep, dark cave. Fergus hid inside the cave, hoping he'd be safe from the monster there.

"Are you getting all of this, Fergus?" Zeke asked.

"I'm trying," Fergus said. He was drawing as fast as he could.

"Then Fergus heard a noise. His whiskers trembled and his fur stood on end. Had the monster found him? Fergus turned on his flashlight and saw a whole family of hungry monsters! The biggest monster grabbed Fergus in its claws and."

Fergus finished his drawing and looked up. "And what?"

"That's it," Zeke said. "I am out of words."

"That is not a very good ending," Fergus said.

"One hundred is not very many words," Zeke said.

"We could revise to make it shorter," Fergus suggested. "Then we'd have room for a happy ending."

Zeke shook his head. "I'm tired of this story. We need a different idea."

"But tomorrow is the one hundredth day of school," Fergus said as the class got ready to go home. "We are out of time!"

"Don't worry," Zeke said. "We'll come up with something after everyone is gone."

"Are you sure?" Fergus asked.

"Positive," Zeke promised. "One hundred percent."

CHAPTER 4

NINETY-NINE AND A HALF CHEESE PUFFS

After the children left, Fergus and Zeke climbed out of their cage to explore.

"There must be one hundred of something in our classroom," Fergus said.

First they checked Miss Maxwell's desk.

"I found some paper clips!" Zeke called.

But when he counted, there were only seventy.

"How about crayons?" said Fergus. "Or pencils? Or something from the first-aid kit?"

But there were only sixty-four crayons in Neela's crayon box . . .

forty-one pencils in the sharing jar . . .

and fifty-two bandages in the first-aid kit.

"It's impossible to find one hundred of anything!" Fergus looked around the room. "And now we have made one hundred messes."

"It's okay," Zeke said. He was nibbling a cheese puff. "We still have time to search. And time to clean up."

"Zeke?" Fergus said. "Where did you get that cheese puff?"

Zeke didn't answer. Fergus ran to the shelf with the hundredth-day projects. When he counted Lucy's cheese puffs, there were only ninety-nine.

"Zeke!" Fergus grabbed the cheese puff. "You almost ruined Lucy's project." Fergus climbed up to the project shelf and put the cheese puff back.

Zeke shrugged. "Searching made me hungry." Then he pointed to Fergus's feet. "And searching made you messy. Did you step in something?"

Fergus looked down. His paws were blue. And he had left blue tracks all over the floor. "Now we have made an even bigger mess!" Fergus said.

"Yes," Zeke said. "And we also have a project!" He grabbed a piece of paper. "Jump on here, Fergus!"

Fergus jumped.

"Again!" Zeke said.

Fergus jumped and looked back. There were blue paw prints behind him. "We do have a project!" Fergus said. "One hundred mouse prints!"

"Are you going to keep jumping on two feet?" Zeke asked. "Then you will only need to jump fifty times. Two times fifty is one hundred. And you've already made four prints!"

Zeke counted by twos while Fergus jumped.

"Six . . . eight . . ."

Fergus had to dip his feet in the paint a few times before he finished.

"Ninety-six . . . ninety-eight . . . one hundred!"

Fergus and Zeke put the paper by their cage to dry. Then they cleaned up all their messes. They climbed into their cage just as the children arrived.

"Happy one hundredth day of school!"
said Miss Maxwell. "Please make sure your
projects are ready to share at our party."

Jake set up a poster board with one hundred pennies taped to it.

Emma folded her one hundredth paper airplane and arranged them in groups of ten.

Neela steadied her tower of one hundred blocks.

Will put on a fancy hat he'd made, with one hundred buttons sewn all over it.

And Lucy recounted her cheese puffs. "Ninety-eight . . . ninety-nine . . . one hundred!"

(She didn't notice that one had been nibbled.)

Emma even brought Fergus and Zeke a special treat for the party—one hundred sunflower seeds!

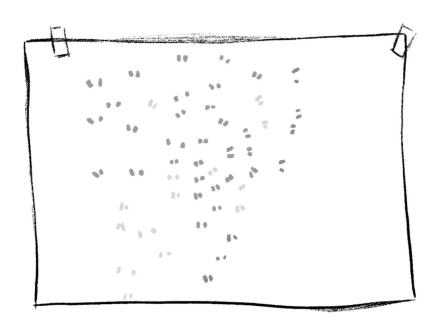

"Miss Maxwell, look!" Emma said. "Fergus and Zeke made a painting, too!"

"Oh dear," Miss Maxwell said. "They must have gotten into our paint. But it looks like they're cleaned up now."

Emma looked more closely at the paw prints, counting silently. "One hundred exactly! Good job, mice!" She smiled and put the sunflower seeds in their cage.

Zeke grabbed a seed, but Fergus said, "Wait! Maybe we should save these so we have a project for next year."

Zeke shook his head. "We will have better ideas by then." He popped the seed into his mouth. "A whole year is a very long time when you're waiting for snacks. And one hundred sunflower seeds are way too delicious for that."